Joshua, Helmut, and Bethlehem

Michelle O. Donovan

Illustrations by Marion Aitken

iUniverse, Inc.
Bloomington

Joshua, Helmut, and Bethlehem

iUniverse books may be ordered through booksellers or by contacting:

iUniverse
1663 Liberty Drive
Bloomington, IN 47403
www.iuniverse.com
1-800-Authors (1-800-288-4677)

Because of the dynamic nature of the Internet, any web addresses or links contained in this book may have changed since publication and may no longer be valid. The views expressed in this work are solely those of the author and do not necessarily reflect the views of the publisher, and the publisher hereby disclaims any responsibility for them.

Any people depicted in stock imagery provided by Thinkstock are models, and such images are being used for illustrative purposes only.

Certain stock imagery © Thinkstock.

ISBN: 978-1-4620-5867-9 (sc)
ISBN: 978-1-4620-5868-6 (e)

Library of Congress Control Number: 2011917966

Printed in the United States of America

iUniverse rev. date: 10/28/2011

DEDICATION and THANK YOU

Because I believe what Marian Wright Eldeman said,
"It is children who are God's Presence, Promise and
Hope for mankind."

I dedicate this touching story to my father, Mr. Daniel Lafontan,
who was incarcerated in four concentration camps: Buchenwald,
Mauthausen, Gusen, and Auschwitz. To my marvelous husband,
Mr. George Edwin Donovan. Honesty, courage, and love for his
Savior Jesus Christ were his attributes as a winner in life. I love
you forever, my wonderful George.

To the jewel and rose of my life, my daughter, Sabrina;
my sister, Lyliane Podlesnik; my uncle Roger and aunt
Eliane Laroche;
and Mr. Alan Frederic Davies, who participated in
D-day on the Normandy beaches.

SPECIAL THANKS TO

Mr. Arthur and Mrs. Rosabelle Birch, Mr. Steven and Mrs. Ruth
Simonyi-Gindele, Mr. Philip and Mrs. Mary Broadhead,
Mr. Chad Kamper, Mr. David Hunt,
Mr. George and Mrs. Sheila Klassen, Mr. Frank and Mrs. Debbie
Krznaric, and Dr. Leonard W. Hatlelid.

Their example has inspired me and still guides my steps day after day.

INTRODUCTION

Life is often unpredictable. Such is the story of *Joshua, Helmut, and Bethlehem*, a story filled with surprises and the unexpected. Although we do not usually expect a Jew to also be a Christian, since its beginning when Christianity arose from Judaism, there have been Jewish followers of Jesus. Yet we are surprised. And how surprising it is that a lonely little boy, doomed to destruction in a war of hate, not only survived but also blessed those around him with the love of God.

J OSHUA CROUCHED UNDER A platform of rotten wooden planks. The boards served as a bed for the emaciated occupants of block number six. In this concentration camp, the shack's occupants faced daily torments and almost certain death at the hands of their cruel tormentors. A mere boy, Joshua caught the welcome sight of a tiny gray muzzle, which sported a long, fine mustache. Joshua stretched out his hand as the little mouse emerged from a hole where the building had settled and where a stream of water and mud leaked through the wooden slats. The mouse came to him and nestled in his palm.

OVING AWAY FROM THE hole, Joshua sat on the floor near the edge of the bed made of planks. Hearing a loud whistle, he quickly closed his hand and slipped his treasure into his pocket. A sinister pair of black leather boots appeared at the door of the hut. There stood an officer, whirling a horse whip in his hand. The man, one of the camp chiefs and a terrible executioner, scanned the room with its makeshift pallets. Bending over, he discovered the terrified young boy. Pointing his whip at the little boy, he told his two companions to get the boy out of his hiding place. They pulled him out by his legs.

Standing to his feet, Joshua faced the laughing, cruel man. Trembling with fear, Joshua was unable to keep his thin body from shivering. He felt sure that he was another innocent lamb about to be led to the slaughter. He had seen his companions leave, never to return. He quivered as he thought about dying. Nervously, he gave a gentle squeeze to the gray muzzle clutched in his right hand. The officer told the boy to follow him. They left the somber prison and crossed the grounds soaked from torrential rain. They entered a building set off by itself—the headquarters reserved for the camp's guards and soldiers.

THE SILENT LAD COULD hear his heart beating with terror. Unable to restrain his own body from trembling, Joshua could feel the little mouse, nestled unmoving in his hand. She knew her little master well and remained calm in his pocket, but the boy jumped at the sound of a husky voice calling his name. Looking up, he discovered a man with white hair. Together they walked down a long corridor and reached a room that Joshua knew to be an infirmary. Smiling, the man told Joshua that he was a doctor and asked him how old he was. Swallowing hard, Joshua whispered, "I'm nine years old, sir." Squeezing Joshua's cheek, the doctor said with a shake of his head, "Don't tremble and don't be afraid anymore, my boy. This soldier will take you where you have to go."

Following the soldier, the scared little nine-year-old continued down the same corridor. Soon he found himself in a large bathroom. There a young woman wearing prison garb ordered him to take off his clothes. Complying, he put his clothes in the corner of the room. The young woman helped him to wash himself. After twenty minutes of being scrubbed clean and then freshly clothed in gray flannel pajamas, Joshua was led by the soldier back to the infirmary where the older gentleman asked him to lie down on the bed. Afraid of what might happen if he did not obey the white-haired man, Joshua obediently lay down.

JOSHUA WATCHED NUMBLY AS a needle pierced his skin and blood gushed into a syringe. The old doctor bent and whispered in his ear, "Somebody is going to bring you some food. My dear boy, if you obey, everything will be fine for you. But, let me give you one more piece of advice: *never, never ask any questions.*" Feeling like he had no choice, Joshua neither spoke a word nor moved a muscle. Looking Joshua intently in the face, the doctor said huskily, "You are privileged, my dear boy. You were surely born under a good star." With that, the man left the room.

Now Joshua was left all alone to wonder what would happen to him next. He knew that those who were taken from the dreaded barracks never came back. Just then, he heard a knock on the door and watched as a soldier brought him a tray of food, but he was too distracted to think about eating. When the door was closed, without thinking of what he was doing, Joshua put his hand in his pocket. With a start, he realized that his little friend was gone. As he put the tray of food on the bed, he felt alone, abandoned by Bethlehem, his beloved friend. With his right hand, he wiped tears from his tired eyes, the beautiful eyes of a nine-year-old boy who had seen horrors that surpassed the limits of cruel imagination. Snuggling under the blanket, he fell asleep without knowing what the next day would bring.

Joshua was awakened by the bright yellow glare from the yard lights that guarded the camp like sentinels. The complete silence of the room made him think about his companions in the camp. Even though he could not hear their cries or see their tears of despair, his fear kept pace with the beat of his heart. His face swam with tears as he thought he would never see the gentle Bethlehem again. In dismay, he whispered, "Jesus, my dear Jesus, where are you? Why all of this? Please help me! Help me! I need you!" Magically, he felt something quivering against his hand. "Oh, Bethlehem! Is it really you? How did you find me? I'm so happy, Bethlehem! Please come to me and please don't leave me anymore! Don't make any noise!" With that, as though he was secreting a precious gem, Joshua hid his little treasure near at hand.

For the following two weeks, Joshua underwent the same treatment. One morning, a young woman awakened him. "Quick, quick," she said. "Here are some new clothes for you. Get dressed quickly. Somebody is coming to take you out of the camp." Dressed in his new clothes, Joshua bravely followed the soldier who came for him. Sitting in the backseat of the Kübelwagen, a German military jeep, he watched as the vehicle went through the giant gate, which was surrounded by terrible razor wire.

REMEMBERING THE DOCTOR'S ADVICE, Joshua remained silent and refrained from asking any questions. In his tired mind, he replayed the painful movie of all he had been through. He recalled the day when his mother had been ordered to leave their miserable home in the concentration camp. Joshua had been hiding under the planks on the muddy floor. His mother had thrown over him the only blanket she possessed. She had hoped that her little boy, by the grace of God, would escape the dreadful call. Joshua had survived as a virtual mute, trying to be invisible so that people would forget his presence. Since then, he had shared his daily, slim pittance of a ration with the gray muzzle.

Leaving his memories behind, Joshua watched through the window as the clouds raced the jeep in which he was riding. The jeep rolled along a stone road for about four hours, but the little boy wished it would never stop. Each minute that passed took him farther from his jail and its relentless horror. Finally they stopped before a giant gray gate with iron bars. The driver opened the gate and then got back into the heavy vehicle and proceeded along a driveway between tall green fir trees. After two or three minutes, the jeep stopped in front of a white mansion. The soldier ordered the boy to get out, and then he drove off the way he had come.

A T THE TOP OF the stairs leading to the mansion's front door stood a man, the majordomo, wearing a black suit and white gloves. He smiled at Joshua. He beckoned to Joshua, and they entered the imposing residence together. They walked down a corridor covered in wallpaper decorated with violet flowers. Opening a door, the gentleman whispered in the young boy's ear, "This is your bedroom, Joshua," and left. Light from a high window looked almost playful, splashing the ceiling and walls with many mirrors. An inviting bed was dressed with a blanket embroidered with golden spangles. For a second, Joshua wondered, *Am I dead?* He thought perhaps he was having a dream about heaven. Suddenly, to his astonishment, the little gray muzzle escaped from his pocket and ran under the bed. Thanks to Bethlehem, he knew he was very much alive.

Bending down, Joshua whispered, "Bethlehem, don't run away anymore. Where are you, Bethlehem? Please come back!" Obediently, the little mouse crawled back into the young boy's palm. Joshua was happily putting his treasure in his pocket when a voice through the doorway made his body bounce like a mattress spring, catapulting him to his feet. The new voice asked him, "What are you doing? Tell me who you are calling."

"Nobody!" stammered a terrified Joshua. "I didn't call anybody!" Just then another little boy entered the room. With his halo of blond hair and shining face, Joshua thought he looked like an angel.

THE NEW BOY INTRODUCED himself. "My name is Helmut. I am nine years old." Virtually shouting, he loudly proclaimed, "I am the son of the great General Krugester. My father is a hero. He's fighting the war and protecting our land against the enemy." With a triumphant voice, he continued, "My dad, yes, my dad is a great hero!" Joshua felt his heart sink like a stone. He didn't know what to do or what to say. Helmut shouted again, "I know who you are! Your name is Joshua. Your parents were killed in a car accident when they were on their way home."

The Jewish boy couldn't understand what the new boy was talking about. Joshua thought, *This must be it! I am going to die!* Closing his eyes, he whispered, "Please, Jesus, take me to be with you now. Please, Jesus, I don't want to suffer anymore." Squeezing Bethlehem in his pocket, he added, "Jesus, please bring my friend with me into your kingdom."

The sound of Helmut's voice interrupted Joshua's prayer. "Follow me into the garden," said the German boy. "I will give you some lemonade and explain why you are here." Opening a glass door, they descended a few steps that led into a little park with beautiful flowers and tall, majestic trees. The blond boy offered Joshua some lemonade. Seizing it with trembling hands, he gulped it all down immediately, as though all his good fortune might come to an end in the enchanted garden. The blond boy insisted that Joshua have more. "Would you like more lemonade, Joshua? And I will tell you why you are here in my dad's house."

With that, Helmut began to explain, "I am sick, Joshua. I have a blood disorder. I need transfusions of blood that is compatible with mine. The doctor in your prison found you and sent you here. Our majordomo told me that you were in jail because you were a bad boy, but you promised to do good, so they sent you here to help me with my health." Joshua couldn't understand why Helmut was telling lies about his parents and himself. But, at that moment, what was important was that he was far away from the hell he had endured. Grabbing Joshua's arm and pulling up his shirtsleeve, the blond German boy asked, "Could you show me your tattoo?" The boy's blue eyes discovered a number engraved in Joshua's flesh.

Abruptly, Helmut released his new companion's arm. Those same blue eyes looked deep into the brown eyes of the Jewish boy, and Helmut exclaimed, "You must have done a very bad thing! It is terrible to have something like this on your arm." Joshua did not respond. For the rest of the day, the blond boy plied the reticent dark-haired boy with questions. At six o'clock, the two boys were called to a dining room where a beautiful meal was served. They devoured it as if they were starving.

When eight o'clock and bedtime arrived, the boy with the dark eyes arrived in his bedroom. A blonde woman was already there. "My name is Magda," she said. "I am here to help you. I will be your nurse and guardian. I am responsible for you. Don't try to escape, because if you do, you will die." With a smile, she added, "Don't be afraid. You must have been born under a good star. I don't know your future, but I do know that you are a very special boy." After Joshua was given a warm bath and clothed in blue pajamas, he smiled timidly at his nurse. "Good night, Joshua," Magda said. "Don't be afraid anymore." Then she left the room.

When the door was shut, Joshua got up quickly. Crouching down to look under the bed, he whispered, "Bethlehem, where are you? Bethlehem, come to me!" In a moment, to the joy of her master, a gray muzzle appeared. Talking softly to her, Joshua gave his friend a piece of bread he had managed to hide despite the watchful eyes of his guardians. In the depths of his abyss, the uncertainty of each moment had taught him to survive with the most meager resources in the sordid camp. Having fed his little friend, Joshua fell asleep and slept through the night.

"Good morning! It's seven o'clock," said Magda. She led him to the shower. Joshua loved the warm water running down his back. After his shower, Magda massaged his shoulders with cologne, making Joshua

21

feel truly alive and well. Freshly clothed, he went to meet Helmut, who was waiting anxiously and impatiently. "Good morning, my friend Joshua!" Helmut cried joyfully. The Jewish boy returned the greeting. Helmut asked, "Did you sleep well?" The sound of Helmut's happy voice made Joshua want to live and live and live forever, far from his former prison.

The boys had a good breakfast and then went to the stable. "I want to show you my horse. I want you to learn to ride," said Helmut. "You see," said the German boy, "horses are my passion. They are strong and honest." With his finger, he pointed out a black saddle horse, its coat shining in the sun. "He's mine and I'm very proud of him. His name is Bravo," shouted Helmut. "When I feel sad, I can tell him all my worries. When my father is away from home, I share my solitude with him. He truly understands me. I love my Bravo. Yes, he really understands me."

TWO WEEKS FLEW BY. During the day, Joshua was with Helmut; at nighttime, he slept with his precious Bethlehem. Hope had started to live in Joshua's heart when one morning the doctor he had met in the camp reappeared. All the fear he had felt before came rushing back. He had started to quiver when the older man wrapped his left arm around Joshua's shoulders. "Follow me," he said. "We are going to do a blood test. Don't be afraid. You are protected in this house."

Lying motionless on the infirmary bed with his eyes staring at the ceiling, Joshua thought about the events of the last fifteen days. Perhaps God had wanted to give him a foretaste of heaven. A smile formed on his lips as he thought how beautiful it would be to die now. On the wings of angels, he would reach the dazzling eternal light just as his mother had told him.

She had said, "Joshua, it's the Light of the World and his name is Jesus Christ. He was born on earth more than two thousand years ago. And he died to save humanity." Then Joshua's memory took him back to his father's arms just a few months ago, before they were arrested and sent to the concentration camp. He remembered being baptized to affirm his faith in the Son of God and his dad saying to him, "I am proud of you, my son."

Joshua remembered the verse of Scripture his father had taught him: "For God so loved the world that he gave his one and only Son, that whoever believes in him shall not perish but have eternal life" (John 3:16 NIV). "The Holy Bible inscribed with God's golden words," his father had said, "tells us the secret of happiness. Unfortunately, the human race didn't obey these magic words. Never forget, Joshua, it is not easy, but no matter what happens on earth, we have a Savior beside us every day. We cannot see him, but don't forget, Joshua, he can see us. He is the Magician of Love."

Waking from his dream, Joshua opened his eyes to see the doctor coming toward the bed. He felt the unpleasant prick of the needle penetrating his vein. Then the white-haired doctor said to him, "You are finished for today. My dear boy, if everything goes well, very soon you will give some blood to Helmut." That night, Bethlehem slept nestled in the hand of her little master.

By six o'clock the next morning, the sun was already bright, the tall green fir trees awash in its golden rays. Coming into Joshua's room and clapping her hands, Magda said, "Get up, Joshua. Today you are going to give life to your new friend. We will do a transfusion. Don't be afraid. Everything will be fine for both of you."

When Magda and Joshua came through the infirmary door, Helmut was already there. Smiling at Joshua, he said, "Good morning, my dear friend. I am starting to like you very much." So full of emotion he could not reply, the little Jewish boy could not deny that he also liked Helmut very much. After a good two hours of sleep, the two friends found large glasses of orange juice in front of them. Pancakes and other delights were also devoured by the two boys—one Jewish, the other German.

ANOTHER MONTH PASSED, AND Joshua's dream was still alive. Following their morning visits to the infirmary, the two boys spent the early afternoons studying before going to play in the garden. This was Helmut and Joshua's new life. Then one morning something in the air felt different. A certain nervousness prevailed inside the imposing mansion. The blond German lad ran toward Joshua with shouts of joy. "Joshua! Joshua! My dad will be here tomorrow! You will meet him tomorrow!" His face was beaming with joy. He was dancing in circles, singing, "Joshua! Tomorrow my father will be here!" Joyfully seizing his companion's hand, he dragged him outside, singing louder and louder, "Tomorrow, Joshua, you will meet my dad!"

At seven o'clock the next morning, Joshua took his breakfast alone. The large, spotless, bright kitchen seemed so empty without Helmut. Joshua didn't ask any questions. In the afternoon, he studied again, but this time he was alone. He realized how the little German boy had become his entire universe. That night, he returned to his bedroom. There Magda told him what was happening with Helmut. With the sound of a Viennese waltz coming from the direction of the guest living room, he fell asleep.

After two days, Joshua had to admit how badly he missed Helmut. In his sadness, Joshua poured out his heart to Jesus, his Helper, asking him to protect Helmut and himself against the adversities and misfortunes of life. On Friday afternoon, Magda reappeared and told Joshua the news he had feared: he was going to meet Helmut's dad. Nevertheless, he courageously followed Magda into a vast office where he saw the famous father for the first time. Helmut stood beside his father, pride glowing on his face like a star on a dark night with a full moon.

THE OFFICER, WEARING A pair of black leather boots, was seated behind a large desk. He stood up and stepped forward, stopping in front of Joshua. Looking intently at Joshua, he said, "Destiny sent you to help us, to save the life of the boy I would die for. Only a few people know who you are, and no one else will ever know. But I assure you that whatever happens in the future, you will be safe here in this house. I will always protect the boy who helped my son to live and made him happy." To both boys he said, "You two can go to the garden and play for a while before dinner."

The following Monday, the two boys rushed to the window at the sound of rapid footsteps pounding the pavement. They saw the General, who was cherished by the boy with blond hair, come to a standstill beside a black Citroën. The Citroën roared to life like an angry lion. Before they knew it, the car, followed by a cavalcade of motorcycles rumbling like thunder, had disappeared from sight. Wiping away the tears that were running down his face, Helmut shouted, "My father is the most powerful general in the whole world. I love him! I love him! He will be back soon!"

Choking back his tears, the German boy took Joshua by the hand and pulled him toward the door leading to the garden. He said, "Come with me. I will show you what my father left for us. Come on! Come on, Joshua!" Two sets of eyes filled with wonder at the sight of two pedal cars. In no time at all, the cars were racing about the garden at the hands of a pair of experienced drivers who were laughing with joy.

ANOTHER FOUR MONTHS FLEW by as Joshua tried to hide his wounds in his new world. Knowing that Jesus was helping him, he buried all his previous suffering in the corner of his heart. Helmut was becoming stronger as his health steadily improved. Every month, his father visited the large mansion. The General could see what was happening between Helmut and his new friend. Bonds of a solid friendship were developing between the two nine-year-old boys. He knew they were becoming as inseparable as two brothers. His son was the pride and joy of his life. Since the death of his loving wife at the boy's birth, Helmut had been his treasure, everything the man desired. The General preferred not to think about Joshua. What mattered was that his own son was alive and happy. That was sufficient for him.

As spring and summer were replaced by autumn, Helmut began to doubt the bad rumors about his new friend. Joshua's loyalty, faithfulness, and straightforwardness drew the boys closer. Joshua was part of his entire life and universe. He loved him like a brother. But inevitably, one day Helmut discovered Bethlehem's existence. Joshua truthfully explained to the German boy how, in his misery, the little mouse had become his friend. To talk and dream with her was all he'd had. The inquisitive blue eyes wanted to know more, and he asked, "Why did you call her Bethlehem?"

Holding back tears, Joshua told his friend, "When everything in my life seemed very dark and hopeless, my dad told me, 'Never despair, because there is always a star that will guide you, an invisible Presence who loves you. Even if dark clouds of suffering prevent us from seeing it, that Presence never leaves us. It is a star of promises, forgiveness, and freedom, all bathed in love. The star shows us that a man was born over two thousand years ago in Bethlehem. One day that man died so that the sins of mankind would be forgiven. He gave us the freedom to choose to follow him by doing good and giving love. His name is

Jesus Christ our Lord. He is the Creator of the heavens, the earth, and each of us.'"

Joshua went on, "So in the wretched camp, when I saw that little mouse running between two planks, I remembered that my mother, too, had told me the story of baby Jesus in the manger. When I caught the little mouse, I thought about the star in Bethlehem's sky that told the shepherds that a King was born to save the world and to give humans freedom. I thought how the Lord God is pure love. You see, Helmut, my friend was free in the camp while I was a prisoner. Like the star of Bethlehem, she was free to run where she wanted to go. She represented everything I had lost. That's why, with new hope in my heart, I called her Bethlehem."

Helmut listened intently to every word flowing from Joshua's heart and lips as he continued, "The Bible contains magic words, as valuable as pure gold. You know, my friend, these golden words were meant to guide us through our lives, but many people don't care and don't listen. They hate and do bad things to each other. But this is what our God, the Lord Jesus Christ, commands: 'Love the Lord your God with all your heart and with all your soul and with all your strength and with all your mind;' and, 'Love your neighbor as yourself'" (Luke 10:27 NIV). With that, Joshua stopped talking. He looked at Helmut, overwhelmed with emotion and with tears running down his face. Helmut asked, "Can I hold Bethlehem in my hand?" Joshua nodded.

For the first time in his young life, Helmut began to feel the real significance of the words *love* and *freedom*. That night, Helmut dreamed that he was flying high above the ocean, soaring on the wind with the birds and guided by a shining star. In his dream, he had no more sickness or pain. He was free.

EARLY ON A BEAUTIFUL morning in late September, around six o'clock, the sun was already bright. An impatient black horse was stamping the ground and kicking the gate of its enclosure. In an adjacent stall, a spirited chestnut pawed the ground. Both horses eagerly awaited the two young boys and the promise of an exhilarating adventure.

At the entrance to a glade, where tracks offered the promise of future discoveries, two freedom-loving boys, hair in the wind, began to trot their mounts. Full of vibrant life, the boys were no longer different in nationality. They needed no passports. One was called Joshua, the other Helmut. They were two hearts shaped in communion with one love given by the Creator. After a frantic, wild race, they drew their mounts to a stop for a break under an old tree.

With the horses grazing on fresh grass, Joshua leaned against a giant fir tree. He put his hand in his pocket. Wrapped in Joshua's handkerchief, Bethlehem remained motionless, full of trust in her master. The boy took the little mouse in his hand. Feeling the fresh air, she began to run on his arm. His jaw clenched to hold back his emotions, Joshua held Bethlehem like a precious gem. Helmut whispered, "Do you finally agree, Joshua?" Joshua put Bethlehem down on the moss. The gray muzzle was hesitant. She pointed her nose toward the new smell. Reassured by the fresh air, she slipped into the bushes and disappeared. The two boys had just given Bethlehem the cherished freedom that all mankind hopes to have. Their two hearts beat as one. At that moment, they felt inseparable.

38

Every day for a year, the boys followed the same routine—visits to the infirmary, studies, and long rides with the loyal Bravo. Then one morning, Magda didn't come into Joshua's bedroom as she normally did. The little boy got up and opened his door, not suspecting that what would happen that day would be unforgettable for two young boys. Looking down the staircase, Joshua spied the majordomo and Magda carrying suitcases. They were walking quickly toward the front door. The entire mansion was in a frenzy. As he watched spellbound, Helmut appeared in front of him. Joshua spoke first, "What is going on?"

With tears streaming down his face, the German boy threw his arms around his friend and cried out, "We have to leave! My father lost the war! They told me that you are free, that you can't come with us. Do you understand Joshua, that you are free? But I don't want to lose you! I love you, Joshua!" Helmut kept repeating, "You are my brother! You are my brother! I love you, Joshua!"

The Jewish boy suddenly understood what had happened. In turn he cried out, "I love you too, Helmut! You are my brother! They cannot separate us! We are brothers! We love each other! You are a part of my life, and I am a part of yours! They have to take me with you!" As the boys clung to each other, a pair of black boots approached them and, without a word, a soldier took Helmut from Joshua.

Now Joshua comprehended even more the commotion in the house. He started to scream, "Jesus, where are you? Don't let this happen to Helmut and me! He's the brother I never had." Leaning helplessly against the wall, exhausted with fear and emotion, he remained motionless. He wanted to die. He could hear the motors revving outside, impatient to escape from Helmut and Joshua's house. Little did either boy know that they would not see each other for a very long time.

Sixty years passed after those dramatic and unforgettable events, years of healing wounds silently buried in the corner of the heart. On this magical evening of December 24, tourists from all around the world congregated in Israel. For a few hours, time seemed to hang in the air. Streets were overrun with people rushing along, their eyes flitting from one person to another. Emotion flowed. People felt the love and shared the dazzling joy. On a perfect night, peace and love fairly streamed from the vault of heaven.

A man followed by a lovely blonde woman and two dark-haired boys hurried along in the throng of people. Leaving the main avenue, they proceeded down a small street to an old wooden door. Pushing it open and entering a small church, they stopped in front of a nativity scene. They gazed at the baby Jesus in the manger, at Mary and Joseph, at a little donkey close to the crib, at woolly lambs, and at shepherds on their knees giving thanks and admiration to God's Glory come to earth to save humanity. One of the boys pointed to the star above the manger's straw roof. His grandfather took him by his hand, and all walked down the aisle to find a seat.

The two little boys were laughing and pushing each other. As they were about to be seated in the front row, one of the boys tripped. In the next row, a stranger watching the scene stood up to help the grandfather lift the boy to his feet. "Merry Christmas," said the boy's grandpa as he shook hands with the stranger with blue eyes. "Merry Christmas to you too," said the stranger, becoming drastically pale. Looking with bewilderment at the grandfather and his family, the stranger cried out, piercing the silence of the church, "Joshua! Joshua! It's you! It is you!" In return, the grandpa shouted, "Helmut! Helmut! It's you!" Overcome with emotion, the two men fell into each other's arms.

THE FAMILY COULDN'T UNDERSTAND what was happening. Not knowing what to do or say, they were too stunned to move. They simply stared at the two men crying and hugging each other. Finally, the men began to explain. When Helmut bent over to help the young boy, he had recognized the tattoo on Joshua's outstretched arm. He had never forgotten that day, as a little boy, when he had grabbed his friend's arm. The number etched in Joshua's skin was still vivid in his memory.

Joshua, full of joy, asked, "Helmut! Helmut! Why are you here? This is unbelievable! Unbelievable! What are you doing here? I never knew what happened to you! I have prayed so much for you!" He kept repeating, "This is unbelievable!"

"And I also hoped that you were alive, and I prayed for you too," said the man with the blue eyes. "Many times I prayed, 'May the God of hope fill you with all joy and peace as you trust in him, so that you may overflow with hope by the power of the Holy Spirit'" (Romans 15:13 NIV).

"I know, I know," stuttered Joshua, his face covered with tears. "God's Word encouraged me over the years: 'I am still confident of this: I will see the goodness of the LORD in the land of the living. Wait for the LORD; be strong and take heart and wait for the LORD.'" (Psalm 27:13–14 NIV).

"But why are you here tonight in Israel?" Joshua asked again. With a voice full of love, Helmut replied, "Because of Bethlehem, Joshua! Because of Bethlehem!"

On that December 24 evening, two grown men once again had become two little boys—one called Joshua, the other called Helmut—reunited by the grace of God.

EPILOGUE

IF THE EVENTS JUST related about two boys of mixed race, a tiny mouse, and a terrible war seem too fantastic to be believed, let it be said that they are not more unbelievable than real life itself. They are not more unimaginable, for example, than the real events that befell the author's father, who never recovered from the atrocities of war and died within a year of the war's end, liberating him from the camps. Nor are they stranger or more tender than the author's own experience, as a child bereft of parents, befriending tiny animals in the loneliness of her grandparents' garden.

As to how two grown men, so close as children, might find each other again in Bethlehem after decades of being torn apart, the reader's own imagination may provide the most satisfying answers. Or perhaps it could have happened like this ...

American soldiers found Joshua in the general's mansion just hours after Helmut's family had snatched him away and fled. Because Joshua's parents had both died, Joshua was placed in an orphanage while a search for next of kin was undertaken. Within a few months, his uncle Isaac found him. In 1948, Uncle Isaac took Joshua to a new home in Israel just as that state was being born. In Israel, Joshua met other members of his larger family. Of all his relatives, Joshua was the only follower of

Jesus, but his Jewish family accepted him and loved him anyway. Out of respect for his parents, they never criticized Joshua's Christian faith. In turn, he loved and accepted them.

While at first Joshua could not fathom why God had allowed him to be torn from Helmut, whom he loved as a brother, in time he saw with gratitude that God had used Helmut and his family to rescue him from almost certain death in the camp. He also came to understand that if the fleeing general had taken Joshua along, his life would have immediately been put in peril again, along with that of the general and his whole family.

Joshua grew up to be an engineer, to marry, to raise two children, and to become a proud grandfather, all the while making his home in Israel. Though decades passed, Helmut was never far from his thoughts.

For his part, Helmut's father had fled with his family to Switzerland. To their relief, in a private clinic in that country, Helmut's ailment was cured. The whole experience of his childhood illness and recovery drew him into the field of medicine. He became a pediatrician. Often as he cared for children, he thought of Joshua, who had given his blood to save Helmut's life. Helmut wanted to give back what Joshua had given him. He often wondered if Joshua was still alive and, if so, where he was.

Helmut never married. His career as a doctor allowed him the privilege of traveling widely. And so it was that one Christmas he decided to travel to Bethlehem to celebrate the faith in Jesus he had embraced through the urging of his childhood friend, Joshua. In a million years, he would never have imagined finding Joshua there, but that is exactly what happened!

Once reunited, the two friends knew that they would never again let anything tear them apart.

Editing: Art & Rosabelle Birch.
Art & Rosabelle have invested their lives in Christian ministry. They are the parents of four children, now grown, with children of their own. As a family, they have always loved reading about adventures as well as experiencing them first hand. They see in our beautiful world and in the worlds of the imagination, which writers envision, evidence of the creative power of the Almighty.

Illustrator: Marion Aitken
Marion was born in Zimbabwe, raised in Stratford, Ontario and now makes Ottawa her home.
A graduate of Sheridan College's Illustration program, she currently runs her own creative consulting business and exhibits Fine Art on the side. She loves participating in adventures of all sorts, particularly those involving traveling.

Author: Michelle Donovan.
Michelle was born in France and moved to Canada in 1968. As a child she grew up alone in her grandparent's home. Following her grandfather around his garden, she entertained herself dreaming about adventures.